12.5.79

THE MORNING STAR

BOOKS BY KENNETH REXROTH

POEMS

The Collected Shorter Poems
The Collected Longer Poems
Sky Sea Birds Trees Earth House Beasts Flowers
New Poems
The Phoenix and the Tortoise
The Morning Star

PLAYS

Beyond the Mountains

CRITICISM & ESSAYS

The Alternative Society
American Poetry in the Twentieth Century
Assays
Bird in the Bush
The Classics Revisited
Communalism, from the Neolithic to 1900
The Elastic Retort
With Eye and Ear

TRANSLATIONS

100 Poems from the Chinese
100 More Poems from the Chinese: Love and the Turning Year
Fourteen Poems of O. V. Lubicz-Milosz
Seasons of Sacred Lust: The Selected Poems of Kazuko Shiraishi
    (*with Ikuko Atsumi, John Solt, Carol Tinker, and*
    Yasuyo Morita)
The Burning Heart: Women Poets of Japan
    (*with Ikuko Atsumi*)
The Orchid Boat: The Women Poets of China
    (*with Ling Chung*)
100 French Poems
Poems from the Greek Anthology
100 Poems from the Japanese
100 More Poems from the Japanese
30 Spanish Poems of Love and Exile
Selected Poems of Pierre Reverdy
Li Ch'ing-chao: Complete Poems (*with Ling Chung*)

AUTOBIOGRAPHY

An Autobiographical Novel

EDITOR

An Anthology of Pre-literate Poetry
The Continuum Poetry Series

KENNETH REXROTH

THE MORNING STAR

A New Directions Book

The transcendent, unchanging beauty of nature, the evanescent, mutable lives and loves of man are the twin themes of Kenneth Rexroth's newest collection of poems and translations, *The Morning Star*. The first section, "The Silver Swan—Poems and Translations Written in Kyoto 1974–78," contains a new group of Rexroth's own crystalline glimpses of the natural world as well as translations of Fujiwara no Teika, Yosano Akiko, and the Swedish poet Gunnar Ekelof. Inspired by the tumulus of a "long dead princess" near the 700-year-old farmhouse in which Rexroth and his wife, Carol Tinker, lived during their stay in Kyoto, the second section of this volume, "On Flower Wreath Hill," is a meditation on mortality and

Grateful acknowledgement is made to the various presses that first printed separate sections of this collection: *The Silver Swan* was first published by Copper Canyon Press, Port Townsend, Washington; *On Flower Wreath Hill* by Blackfish Press, Burnaby, British Columbia; and *The Love Poems of Marichiko* by Christopher's Books, Santa Barbara, California.

Acknowledgment is also due to the following publications in which some of the poems in this volume were originally included: *American Poetry Review, Invisible City, Kyoto Review, Poetry Now,* and *Zero.* Some of *The Love Poems of Marichiko* appeared previously in *100 More Poems from the Japanese, New Poems,* and *New Directions in Prose and Poetry 29* all published by New Directions.

Manufactured in the United States of America
First published clothbound and as New Directions Paperbook 490 in 1979
Published simultaneously in Canada by George J. McLeod, Ltd., Toronto

Library of Congress Cataloging in Publication Data

Rexroth, Kenneth, 1905–
  The morning star.

  (A New Directions Book)
  Poems; originally published under their separate titles.
  CONTENTS: The silver swan.—On Flower Wreath Hill.—
The love poems of Marichiko.
  Includes index.
  I. Title.
PS3535.E923A17   1979   811'.5'2   79-14977
ISBN 0-8112-0739-0
ISBN 0-8112-0740-4 pbk.

New Directions Books are published for James Laughlin
by New Directions Publishing Corporation,
80 Eighth Avenue, New York 10011

CONTENTS

The Silver Swan   1

On Flower Wreath Hill   33

The Love Poems of Marichiko   47

NOTES   83

INDEX OF TITLES, FIRST LINES, AND
    AUTHORS TRANSLATED   89

To Carol

THE SILVER SWAN

poems and translations
written in Kyoto 1974–1978

I

for *Ruth Stephan*

Twilit snow,
The last time I saw it
Was with you.
Now you are dead
By your own hand
After great pain.
Twilit snow.

I I

As the full moon rises[*]
The swan sings
In sleep
On the lake of the mind.

I I I

Orange and silver
Twilight over Yoshino.
Then the frosty stars,
Moving like crystals against
The wind from Siberia.

IV

Under the half moon
The field crickets are silent.
Only the cricket
Of the hearth still sings, louder
Still, behind the gas heater.

V

Late night, under the
Low, waning eleventh month
Moon, wild frosted kaki
On the bare branches gleam like
Pearls. Tomorrow they
Will be sweet as the
Honey of Summer.

V I

Asagumori

On the forest path
The leaves fall. In the withered
Grass the crickets sing
Their last songs. Through dew and dusk
I walk the paths you once walked,
My sleeves wet with memory.

VII

Void Only

I cannot escape from you.
When I think I am alone,
I awake to discover
I am lost in the jungle
Of your love, in its darkness
Jewelled with the eyes of unknown
Beasts. I awake to discover
I am a forest ascetic
In the impenetrable
Void only, the single thought
Of which nothing can be said.

VIII

Seven Seven

Can I come to you
When the cowboy comes to the
Weaving girl? No sea is as
Wide as the River of Heaven.

I X

The new moon has reached
The half. It is utterly
Incredible. One
Month ago we were strangers.

X

After Akiko—"Yoru no cho ni"

for *Yasuyo*

In your frost white kimono
Embroidered with bare branches
I walk you home New Year's Eve.
As we pass a street lamp
A few tiny bright feathers
Float in the air. Stars form on
Your wind blown hair and you cry,
"The first snow!"

XI

Late Spring.
Before he goes, the uguisu
Says over and over again
The simple lesson no man
Knows, because
No man can ever learn.

XII

Bride and groom,
The moon shines
Above the typhoon.

XIII

Only the sea mist,
Void only.
Only the rising
Full moon,
Void only.

XIV

Hototogisu—horobirete

The cuckoo's call, though
Sweet in itself, is hard to
Bear, for it cries,
"Perishing! Perishing!"
Against the Spring.

XV

Tsukutsukuboshi

In the month of great heat
The first bell cricket cries.
"It is time to leave."

XVI

New Year

The full moon shines on
The first plum blossoms and opens
The Year of the Dragon.
May happy Dragons
Attend you with gifts of joy.

XVII

An hour before sunrise,
The moon low in the East,
Soon it will pass the sun.
The Morning Star hangs like a
Lamp, beside the crescent,
Above the greying horizon.
The air warm, perfumed,
An unseasonably warm,
Rainy Autumn, nevertheless
The leaves turn color, contour
By contour down the mountains.
I watch the wavering,
Coiling of the smoke of a
Stick of temple incense in
The rays of my reading lamp.
Moonlight appears on my wall
As though I raised it by
Incantation. I go out
Into the wooded garden
And walk, nude, except for my
Sandals, through light and dark banded
Like a field of sleeping tigers.
Our racoons watch me from the
Walnut tree, the opossums
Glide out of sight under the
Woodpile. My dog Ch'ing is asleep.
So is the cat. I am alone
In the stillness before the
First birds wake. The night creatures
Have all gone to sleep. Blackness
Looms at the end of the garden,
An impenetrable cube.
A ray of the Morning Star
Pierces a shaft of moon-filled mist.
A naked girl takes form
And comes toward me—translucent,
Her body made of infinite

Whirling points of light, each one
A galaxy, like clouds of
Fireflies beyond numbering.
Through them, star and moon
Still glisten faintly. She comes
To me on imperceptibly
Drifting air, and touches me
On the shoulder with a hand
Softer than silk. She says
"Lover, do you know what Heart
You have possessed?"
Before I can answer, her
Body flows into mine, each
Corpuscle of light merges
With a corpuscle of blood or flesh.
As we become one the world
Vanishes. My self vanishes.
I am dispossessed, only
An abyss without limits.
Only dark oblivion
Of sense and mind in an
Illimitable Void.
Infinitely away burns
A minute red point to which
I move or which moves to me.
Time fades away. Motion is
Not motion. Space becomes Void.
A ruby fire fills all being.
It opens, not like a gate,
Like hands in prayer that unclasp
And close around me.
Then nothing. All senses ceased.
No awareness, nothing,
Only another kind of knowing
Of an all encompassing
Love that has consumed all being.
Time has had a stop.
Space is gone.
Grasping and consequence

Never existed.
The aeons have fallen away.

Suddenly I am standing
In my garden, nude, bathed in
The hot brilliance of the new
Risen sun—star and crescent gone into light.

XVIII

Midnight, the waning moon
Of midsummer glows
From the raindrops on
The first flowers of Autumn.

XIX

The drowned moon plunges
Through a towering surf
Of storm clouds, and momently
The wet leaves glitter.
Moment by moment an owl cries.
Rodents scurry, building
Their winter nests, in the moments of dark.

XX

Plovers cry in the
Dark over the high moorland,
The overtones of the sea,
Calling deep into the land.

XXI

Long past midnight, I walk out
In the garden after a
Hot bath, in yukata
And clogs. I feel no cold.
But the leaves have all fallen
From the fruit trees and the
Kaki hang there alone
Filled with frosty moonlight.
Suddenly I am aware
There is no sound
Not of insects nor of frogs nor of birds
Only the slow pulse of
An owl marking time for the silence.

XXII

Bright in the East
The morrow pure and pale
This hour, this is our last hourglass.
The parting forever of lovers
Is a double suicide
Of the consciousness.
By tens and thousands the stars go out.

XXIII

All This to Pass Never to Be Again

for *Christina, Carol, and Kenneth*

We feed the blue jays
Peanuts from our hands.
As the sun sets, the quarter moon
Shows pale as snow in the orange sky.
While we eat our high cuisine,
The moon, deep in the sky
Moves again in the pool,
And makes it deep as the sky
Where Scorpio moves with it,
Past the South. The crossroads
Of heaven glimmer with billions
Of worlds. The night cools.
We go indoors and talk
Of the wisdom and the
Insoluble problems of India.
Late in the night,
After the moon is down,
Coyotes sing on the hills.
How easy it is to put together
A poem of life lived
Simply and beautifully.
How steadily, as the age grows old,
The opportunity to do so narrows.

XXIV

Flowers sleep by the window.
The lamp holds fast the light.
Carelessly the window holds back the darkness outside.
The empty picture frames exhibit their contents,
And reflect the motionless flies on the walls.

The flowers hold themselves up against the night.
The lamp spins the night.
The cat in the corner spins the wool of sleep.
On the fire now and then the coffeepot snores with content.
Silent children play with words on the ground.

Set the white table. Wait for someone
Whose footsteps will never come up the stairs.

A train bores through the distant silence,
Never revealing the secret of things.
Destiny counts the clock ticks in decimals.

Gunnar Ekelof

XXV

October Mirror

Nerves grind quietly in the twilight
That flows grey and quiet past the window,
When red flowers fade quiet in the twilight
And the lamp sings to itself in the corner.

Silence drinks the quiet Autumn rain
Which no longer means anything to the harvest.
The hands warm their knuckles.
The eyes gaze quiet at the fading embers.

Gunnar Ekelof

XXVI

Equation

Only truth can explain your eyes
That sow stars in the vault of heaven,
Where the clouds float through a field of tones

(The flowers which are born out of nothing,
When your eyes make fate so simple,
And the stars fly away from the hive
In the blue-green waiting room of heaven)

And explain your rapport with destiny.

Gunnar Ekelof

XXVII

I look around,
No cherry blossoms,
No maple leaves,
Only a narrow inlet,
A thatched hut,
In the Autumn evening.

Fujiwara no Teika

XXVIII

I wonder if you can know
In the island of
Your heart, deprived of
Food, unable to escape,
How utterly banished I am.

Yosano Akiko

ON FLOWER WREATH HILL

For Yasuyo Morita

I

An aging pilgrim on a
Darkening path walks through the
Fallen and falling leaves, through
A forest grown over the
Hilltop tumulus of a
Long dead princess, as the
Moonlight grows and the daylight
Fades and the Western Hills turn
Dim in the distance and the
Lights come on, pale green
In the streets of the hazy city.

II

Who was this princess under
This mound overgrown with trees
Now almost bare of leaves?
Only the pine and cypress
Are still green. Scattered through the
Dusk are orange wild kaki on
Bare branches. Darkness, an owl
Answers the temple bell. The
Sun has passed the crossroads of
Heaven.
      There are more leaves on
The ground than grew on the trees.
I can no longer see the
Path; I find my way without
Stumbling; my heavy heart has
Gone this way before. Until
Life goes out memory will
Not vanish, but grow stronger
Night by night.
           Aching nostalgia—
In the darkness every moment
Grows longer and longer, and
I feel as timeless as the
Two thousand year old cypress.

III

The full moon rises over
Blue Mount Hiei as the orange
Twilight gives way to dusk.
Kamo River is full with
The first rains of Autumn, the
Water crowded with colored
Leaves, red maple, yellow gingko,
On dark water, like Chinese
Old brocade. The Autumn haze
Deepens until only the
Lights of the city remain.

I V

No leaf stirs. I am alone
In the midst of a hundred
Empty mountains. Cicadas,
Locusts, katydids, crickets,
Have fallen still, one after
Another. Even the wind
Bells hang motionless. In the
Blue dusk, widely spaced snowflakes
Fall in perfect verticals.
Yet, under my cabin porch,
The thin, clear Autumn water
Rustles softly like fine silk.

V

This world of ours, before we
Can know its fleeting sorrows,
We enter it through tears.
Do the reverberations
Of the evening bell of
The mountain temple ever
Totally die away?
Memory echoes and reechoes
Always reinforcing itself.
No wave motion ever dies.
The white waves of the wake of
The boat that rows away into
The dawn, spread and lap on the
Sands of the shores of all the world.

VI

Clustered in the forest around
The royal tumulus are
Tumbled and shattered gravestones
Of people no one left in
The world remembers. For the
New Year the newer ones have all been cleaned
And straightened and each has
Flowers or at least a spray
Of bamboo and pine.
It is a great pleasure to
Walk through fallen leaves, but
Remember, you are alive,
As they were two months ago.

VII

Night shuts down the misty mountains
With fine rain. The seventh day
Of my seventieth year,
Seven-Seven-Ten, my own
Tanabata, and my own
Great Purification. Who
Crosses in midwinter from
Altair to Vega, from the
Eagle to the Swan, under the earth,
Against the sun? Orion,
My guardian king, stands on
Kegonkyoyama.
So many of these ancient
Tombs are the graves of heroes
Who died young. The combinations
Of the world are unstable
By nature. Take it easy.
Nirvana.
Change rules the world forever.
And man but a little while.

VIII

Oborozuki,
Drowned Moon,
The half moon is drowned in mist
Its hazy light gleams on leaves
Drenched with warm mist. The world
Is alive tonight. I am
Immersed in living protoplasm,
That stretches away over
Continents and seas. I float
Like a child in the womb. Each
Cell of my body is
Penetrated by a
Strange electric life. I glow
In the dark with the moon drenched
Leaves, myself a globe
Of St. Elmo's fire.

I move silently on the
Wet forest path that circles
The shattered tumulus.
The path is invisible.
I am only a dim glow
Like the tumbled and broken
Gravestones of forgotten men
And women that mark the way.
I sit for a while on one
Tumbled sotoba and listen
To the conversations of
Owls and nightjars and tree frogs.
As my eyes adjust to the
Denser darkness I can see
That my seat is a cube and
All around me are scattered
Earth, water, air, fire, ether.
Of these five elements
The moon, the mist, the world, man
Are only fleeting compounds

Varying in power, and
Power is only insight
Into the void—the single
Thought that illuminates the heart.
The heart's mirror hangs in the void.

Do there still rest in the broken
Tumulus ashes and charred
Bones thrown in a corner by
Grave robbers, now just as dead?
She was once a shining flower
With eyebrows like the first night's moon,
Her white face, her brocaded
Robes perfumed with cypress and
Sandalwood; she sang in the Court
Before the Emperor, songs
Of China and Turkestan.
She served him wine in a cup
Of silver and pearls, that gleamed
Like the moonlight on her sleeves.
A young girl with black hair
Longer than her white body—
Who never grew old. Now owls
And nightjars sing in a mist
Of silver and pearls.

The wheel
Swings and turns counterclockwise.
The old graspings live again
In the new consequences.
Yet, still, I walk this same path
Above my cabin in warm
Moonlit mist, in rain, in
Autumn wind and rain of maple
Leaves, in spring rain of cherry
Blossoms, in new snow deeper
Than my clogs. And tonight in
Midsummer, a night enclosed
In an infinite pearl.
Ninety-nine nights over

Yamashina Pass, and the
Hundredth night and the first night
Are the same night. The night
Known prior to consciousness,
Night of ecstasy, night of
Illumination so complete
It cannot be called perceptible.

Winter, the flowers sleep on
The branches. Spring, they awake
And open to probing bees.
Summer, unborn flowers sleep
In the young seeds ripening
In the fruit. The mountain pool
Is invisible in the
Glowing mist. But the mist-drowned
Moon overhead is visible
Drowned in the invisible water.

Mist-drenched, moonlit, the sculpture
Of an orb spider glitters
Across the path. I walk around
Through the bamboo grass. The mist
Dissolves everything else, the
Living and the dead, except
This occult mathematics of light.
Nothing moves. The wind that blows
Down the mountain slope from
The pass and scatters the spring
Blossoms and the autumn leaves
Is still tonight. Even the
Spider's net of jewels has ceased
To tremble. I look back at
An architecture of pearls
And silver wire. Each minute
Droplet reflects a moon, as
Once did the waterpails of
Matsukaze and Murasame.

And I realize that this
Transcendent architecture
Lost in the forest where no one passes
Is itself the Net of Indra,
The compound infinities of infinities,
The Flower Wreath,
Each universe reflecting
Every other, reflecting
Itself from every other,
And the moon the single thought
That populates the Void.
The night grows still more still. No
Sound at all, only a flute
Playing soundlessly in the
Circle of dancing gopis.

THE LOVE POEMS OF
MARICHIKO

translated by Kenneth Rexroth

To Marichiko
Kenneth Rexroth

To Kenneth Rexroth
Marichiko

I

I sit at my desk.
What can I write to you?
Sick with love,
I long to see you in the flesh.
I can write only,
"I love you. I love you. I love you."
Love cuts through my heart
And tears my vitals.
Spasms of longing suffocate me
And will not stop.

I I

If I thought I could get away
And come to you,
Ten thousand miles would be like one mile.
But we are both in the same city
And I dare not see you,
And a mile is longer than a million miles.

III

Oh the anguish of these secret meetings
In the depth of night,
I wait with the shoji open.
You come late, and I see your shadow
Move through the foliage
At the bottom of the garden.
We embrace—hidden from my family.
I weep into my hands.
My sleeves are already damp.
We make love, and suddenly
The fire watch loom up
With clappers and lantern.
How cruel they are
To appear at such a moment.
Upset by their apparition,
I babble nonsense
And can't stop talking
Words with no connection.

I V

You ask me what I thought about
Before we were lovers.
The answer is easy.
Before I met you
I didn't have anything to think about.

V

Autumn covers all the world
With Chinese old brocade.
The crickets cry, "We mend old clothes."
They are more thrifty than I am.

VI

Just us.
In our little house
Far from everybody,
Far from the world,
Only the sound of water over stone.
And then I say to you,
"Listen. Hear the wind in the trees."

VII

Making love with you
Is like drinking sea water.
The more I drink
The thirstier I become,
Until nothing can slake my thirst
But to drink the entire sea.

VIII

A single ray in the dawn,
The bliss of our love
Is incomprehensible.
No sun shines there, no
Moon, no stars, no lightning flash,
Not even lamplight.
All things are incandescent
With love which lights up all the world.

IX

You wake me,
Part my thighs, and kiss me.
I give you the dew
Of the first morning of the world.

X

Frost covers the reeds of the marsh.
A fine haze blows through them,
Crackling the long leaves.
My full heart throbs with bliss.

XI

Uguisu sing in the blossoming trees.
Frogs sing in the green rushes.
Everywhere the same call
Of being to being.
Somber clouds waver in the void.
Fishing boats waver in the tide.
Their sails carry them out.
But ropes, as of old, woven
With the hair of their women,
Pull them back
Over their reflections on the green depths,
To the ports of love.

XII

Come to me, as you come
Softly to the rose bed of coals
Of my fireplace
Glowing through the night-bound forest.

XIII

Lying in the meadow, open to you
Under the noon sun,
Hazy smoke half hides
My rose petals.

XIV

On the bridges
And along the banks
Of Kamo River, the crowds
Watch the character "Great"
Burst into red fire on the mountain
And at last die out.
Your arm about me,
I burn with passion.
Suddenly I realize—
It is life I am burning with.
These hands burn,
Your arm about me burns,
And look at the others,
All about us in the crowd, thousands,
They are all burning—
Into embers and then into darkness.
I am happy.
Nothing of mine is burning.

XV

Because I dream
Of you every night,
My lonely days
Are only dreams.

XVI

Scorched with love, the cicada
Cries out. Silent as the firefly,
My flesh is consumed with love.

XVII

Let us sleep together here tonight.
Tomorrow, who knows where we will sleep?
Maybe tomorrow we will lie in the fields,
Our heads on the rocks.

XVIII

Fires
Burn in my heart.
No smoke rises.
No one knows.

XIX

I pass the day tense, day-
Dreaming of you. I relax with joy
When in the twilight I hear
The evening bells ring from temple to temple.

XX

Who is there? Me.
Me who? I am me. You are you.
You take my pronoun,
And we are us.

XXI

The full moon of Spring
Rises from the Void,
And pushes aside the net
Of stars, a pure crystal ball
On pale velvet, set with gems.

XXII

This Spring, Mercury
Is farthest from the sun and
Burns, a ray of light,
In the glow of dawn
Over the uncountable
Sands and waves of the
Illimitable ocean.

XXIII

I wish I could be
Kannon of eleven heads
To kiss you, Kannon
Of the thousand arms,
To embrace you forever.

XXIV

I scream as you bite
My nipples, and orgasm
Drains my body, as if I
Had been cut in two.

XXV

Your tongue thrums and moves
Into me, and I become
Hollow and blaze with
Whirling light, like the inside
Of a vast expanding pearl.

It is the time when
The wild geese return. Between
The setting sun and
The rising moon, a line of
Brant write the character "heart."

XXVII

As I came from the
Hot bath, you took me before
The horizontal mirror
Beside the low bed, while my
Breasts quivered in your hands, my
Buttocks shivered against you.

XXVIII

Spring is early this year.
Laurel, plums, peaches,
Almonds, mimosa,
All bloom at once. Under the
Moon, night smells like your body.

XXIX

Love me. At this moment we
Are the happiest
People in the world.

XXX

Nothing in the world is worth
One sixteenth part of the love
Which sets free our hearts.
Just as the Morning Star in
The dark before dawn
Lights up the world with its ray,
So love shines in our hearts and
Fills us with glory.

XXXI

Some day in six inches of
Ashes will be all
That's left of our passionate minds,
Of all the world created
By our love, its origin
And passing away.

XXXII

I hold your head tight between
My thighs, and press against your
Mouth, and float away
Forever, in an orchid
Boat on the River of Heaven.

XXXIII

I cannot forget
The perfumed dusk inside the
Tent of my black hair,
As we awoke to make love
After a long night of love.

XXXIV

Every morning, I
Wake alone, dreaming my
Arm is your sweet flesh
Pressing my lips.

XXXV

The uguisu sleeps in the bamboo grove,
One night a man traps her in a bamboo trap,
Now she sleeps in a bamboo cage.

XXXVI

I am sad this morning.
The fog was so dense,
I could not see your shadow
As you passed my shoji.

XXXVII

Is it just the wind
In the bamboo grass,
Or are you coming?
At the least sound
My heart skips a beat.
I try to suppress my torment
And get a little sleep,
But I only become more restless.

XXXVIII

I waited all night.
By midnight I was on fire.
In the dawn, hoping
To find a dream of you,
I laid my weary head
On my folded arms,
But the songs of the waking
Birds tormented me.

XXXIX

Because I can't stop,
Even for a moment's rest from
Thinking of you,
The obi which wound around me twice,
Now goes around me three times.

XL

As the wheel follows the hoof
Of the ox that pulls the cart,
My sorrow follows your footsteps,
As you leave me in the dawn.

XLI

On the mountain,
Tiring to the feet,
Lost in the fog, the pheasant
Cries out, seeking her mate.

XLII

How many lives ago
I first entered the torrent of love,
At last to discover
There is no further shore.
Yet I know I will enter again and again.

XLIII

Two flowers in a letter.
The moon sinks into the far off hills.
Dew drenches the bamboo grass.
I wait.
Crickets sing all night in the pine tree.
At midnight the temple bells ring.
Wild geese cry overhead.
Nothing else.

XLIV

The disorder of my hair
Is due to my lonely sleepless pillow.
My hollow eyes and gaunt cheeks
Are your fault.

XLV

When in the Noh theater
We watched Shizuka Gozen
Trapped in the snow,
I enjoyed the tragedy,
For I thought,
Nothing like this
Will ever happen to me.

XLVI

Emitting a flood of light,
Flooded with light within,
Our love was dimmed by
Forces which came from without.

XLVII

How long, long ago.
By the bridge at Uji,
In our little boat,
We swept through clouds of fireflies.

XLVIII

Now the fireflies of our youth
Are all gone,
Thanks to the efficient insecticides
Of our middle age.

XLIX

Once again I hear
The first frogs sing in the pond.
I am overwhelmed by the past.

L

In the park a crow awakes
And cries out under the full moon,
And I awake and sob
For the years that are gone.

L I

Did you take me because you loved me?
Did you take me without love?
Or did you just take me
To experiment on my heart?

L I I

Once I shone afar like a
Snow-covered mountain.
Now I am lost like
An arrow shot in the dark.
He is gone and I must learn
To live alone and
Sleep alone like a hermit
Buried deep in the jungle.
I shall learn to go
Alone, like the unicorn.

LIII

Without me you can only
Live at random like
A falling pachinko ball.
I am your wisdom.

LIV

Did a cuckoo cry?
I look out, but there is only dawn and
The moon in its final night.
Did the moon cry out
Horobirete! Horobirete!
Perishing! Perishing!

L V

The night is too long to the sleepless.
The road is too long to the footsore.
Life is too long to a woman
Made foolish by passion.
Why did I find a crooked guide
On the twisted paths of love?

L V I

This flesh you have loved
Is fragile, unstable by nature
As a boat adrift.
The fires of the cormorant fishers
Flare in the night.
My heart flares with this agony.
Do you understand?
My life is going out.
Do you understand?
My life.
Vanishing like the stakes
That hold the nets against the current
In Uji River, the current and the mist
Are taking me.

LVII

Night without end. Loneliness.
The wind has driven a maple leaf
Against the shoji. I wait, as in the old days,
In our secret place, under the full moon.
The last bell crickets sing.
I found your old love letters,
Full of poems you never published.
Did it matter? They were only for me.

LVIII

Half in a dream
I become aware
That the voices of the crickets
Grow faint with the growing Autumn.
I mourn for this lonely
Year that is passing
And my own being
Grows fainter and fades away.

LIX

I hate this shadow of a ghost
Under the full moon.
I run my fingers through my greying hair,
And wonder, have I grown so thin?

LX

Chilled through, I wake up
With the first light. Outside my window
A red maple leaf floats silently down.
What am I to believe?
Indifference?
Malice?
I hate the sight of coming day
Since that morning when
Your insensitive gaze turned me to ice
Like the pale moon in the dawn.

NOTES

On Flower Wreath Hill

In 1974–75, we lived in Kyoto in an embayment of Higashi-yama, the Eastern Hills, in a seven hundred year old farm house. The range, which rises directly above the easternmost long street of the city, culminates in Mt. Hiei. It is almost entirely forest and wildlife reserve because scattered all through it are temples and tombs and cemeteries. Our street led up to Yamashina Pass and across the street from our house a shoulder of the range rose abruptly to a little plateau on which long ago had been built the tumulus of a princess which now is only an irregular heap of low mounds covered with trees. Behind it is the complex of Shingon Temples called Sennuji, which includes a large building in which are stored the ashes of former emperors. The Japanese seldom bury the dead, and the tumulus age was of very short duration at the beginning of Japanese history, although it resulted in immense keyhole shaped mounds, one of them of greater bulk than the Great Pyramid of Gizeh, keyhole shaped and surrounded by a moat. The one mentioned in the poem had been a far more modest structure. Mt. Hiei is the site of the founding temples of Tendai and once, before they were all slaughtered by Nobunaga, contained sixty thousand monks at least. Today there are still many monasteries—but also an amusement park. Kamo River flows close to the edge of the mountains.

The second and third verses of Part II are a conflation of well-known classic Japanese poems, and Part V is entirely so.

Tanabata is Seven-Seven, the seventh day of the seventh month, when the Cowboy, Altair, crosses the Milky Way to lie for one night only with the Weaving Girl, Vega. Magpies link wings and form a bridge for him to cross, but there are many Chinese and Japanese dawn poems which would indicate that he rowed himself back.

Kegonkyo (Flower Wreath Sutra) is the Avatamsaka Sutra, by far the most profound and the most mystical of the sutras of Mahavana.

Before he entered Paranirvana, Buddha said, "The combinations of the world are unstable by nature. Monks, strive without ceasing."

St. Elmo's fires are the glowing balls of atmospheric electricity that usually appear as tips of light on the extremities of pointed objects such as church towers or airplane wings during stormy weather.

Important Japanese graves or family burial lots (only the ashes are buried) are often marked by a stupa (Japanese: *sotoba*) consisting of four and sometimes five stones, a cube, a sphere, a lune, a triangle, and sometimes a little shape on top of the triangle. Amongst other things, they symbolize the elements: earth, water, air, fire, and what we used to call ether. Unstable by nature, they do not take many decades to fall apart. There is a Mahayana doctrine, Sunyata, that ultimate reality is Void Only and what seems like reality are only fleeting compounds.

The third verse paragraph of Part VIII begins the possession by Ono no Komachi continued in the next paragraph, and there are many echoes of the three great Noh plays on Komachi, the greatest Japanese woman poet.

The fifth paragraph opens with an echo of a commentary on the Lotus Sutra; but with the orb spider's net, it becomes a poem of the Flower Wreath Sutra, known in Hinduism as the Net of Indra. Matsukaze and Murasame were two lovers of a prince exiled to the shore of Suma. They were salt girls who evaporated sea water over burning dried seaweed and driftwood, and who saw the moon one night after the prince had left, each in her own water pail or pails. There is a very beautiful Noh play on the subject, and they are common dolls. As dolls, they each carry two pails on a yoke and the classic dance with the yoked pails is one of the most beautiful.

The gopis are the nineteen thousand milkmaids who dance to Krishna's flute. His flute music connects true reality and the gopis, who dance and become Real. Music is being, but behind being is Ishvara, what Western philosophy would call the Absolute behind all absolutes. Kabbalah calls it the Ayn Soph and Buddhism the Adi-buddha. As the music enters her, and she enters the dance, each gopi knows that she is Radha, the beloved of Krishna, his Shakti, his Power, or his Prajna, his Wisdom. He is the avatar of Vishnu, and power and wisdom are the same. The Vishnulila, the play of Vishnu with the world of illusion.

Modern stuffy Indian pundits say that Krishna didn't really make love to nineteen thousand milkmaids. He knew by heart 19,000 slokas of the Vedas.

Flower Wreath Hill is also a Chinese and Japanese euphemism for a cemetery.

The Love Poems of Marichiko

Marichiko is the pen name of a contemporary young woman who lives near the temple of Marishi-ben in Kyoto.

Marishi-ben is an Indian, pre-Aryan, goddess of the dawn who is a bodhisattva in Buddhism and patron of geisha, prostitutes, women in childbirth, and lovers, and, in another aspect, once of samurai. Few temples or shrines to her or even statues exist in Japan, but her presence is indicated by statues, often in avenues like sphinxes, of wild boars, who also draw her chariot. She has three faces: the front of compassion; one side, a sow; the other a woman in ecstasy. She is a popular, though hidden, deity of tantric, Tachigawa Shingon. As the Ray of Light, the Shakti, or Prajna, the Power or Wisdom of Vairocana (the primordial Buddha, Dainichi Nyorai), she is seated on his lap in sexual bliss, Myogo—the Morning Star.

Marichiko writes me, now that I am doing so many of her poems, in reference to the note on her in my *One Hundred More Poems from the Japanese*, "Although Marichi is the Shakti, or power, of the Indian god of the sun, she is the Prajna, or wisdom, of Dainichi Nyorai. Dainichi means Great Sun, but he is that only in a metaphorical sense, the Illuminator of the compound infinity of infinities of universes. The Buddhas and Bodhisattvas of Mahayana do not have Shaktis as consorts, for the simple reason that there is no such thing as power in Buddhism. Power is ignorance and grasping. With illumination, it turns into wisdom."

Notice, that like the English seventeenth-century poet Rochester, many of her poems turn religious verse into erotic, and she also turns traditional geisha songs into visionary poems. They therefore bear comparison with Persian Sufi poets, Hafidh, Attar, Sa'adi, and others, and with the Arab, Ibn el Arabi—with all of whom she is familiar in translation.

The series of poems, as should be obvious, form a sort of little novel and recall the famous *Diary of Izumi Shikibu* without the connecting prose. Notice that the sex of the lover is ambiguous.

Poem IV. Echoes Fujiwara no Atsutada, "Ai minto no."

Poem V. Narihira compares the leaf covered water of Tatsuta River to Chinese old brocade.

Poem VI. Echoes several "honeymoon houses," the modern one by Yosano Akiko.

Poem VII. Echoes a passage in the *Katha Upanishad*.

Poem VIII. Echoes a passage in the *Katha Upanishad*.

Poem XI. The uguisu, often translated "nightingale," is not a nightingale and does not sing at night. It is the Japanese bush warbler, *Horeites cantans cantans*, or *Cettia diphone*.

Poem XIV. Refers to the Festival, Daimonji Okuribi, sending of the dead back to heaven, when huge bonfires in the shape of characters are lit on the mountain sides around Kyoto. There is a paraphrase of Buddha's Fire Sermon and a paraphrase of Rilke's paraphrase of that.

Poem XVI. Based on a geisha song in many forms.

Poem XVII. Either the poem on Hitomaro's (Japan's greatest poet—b.?–d.739) death or his own poem on a friend's death.

Poem XX. This poem, though syntactically barely possible, would be inconceivable in classical Japanese.

Poem XXI. There is an implied reference to the doctrine of Void Only and then to the Avatamsaka Sutra (Kegongyo) as the Net of Indra.

Poem XXII. The ray of light of the Morning Star—Marishiten—Myogo.

Poem XXIII. Both forms of Kannon (Avalokitesvara) are common statues. Sanjusangendo, across from the Kyoto Art Museum, is a hall of over a thousand such, each very slightly different.

Poem XXVI. Brant, *Branta bernicia* is Japanese Koku-gan, are small, dark geese, who winter in the north of Honshu, the main island. Unlike many birds of the family, they do not fly in arrow formations, but in an irregular line.

Poem XXVII. The horizontal mirror is a narrow mirror, closed by sliding panels, alongside the bed in many Japanese inns (ryokan). Shunga erotic woodblock prints, representing them, are usually called "seen through the slats of a bamboo screen" by Westerners—Japanese until recent times had nothing resembling our venetian blinds.

Poem XXX. Echoes the Buddhist sutra Itivuttaka, III, 7.

Poem XXXI. Echoes the Buddhist sutra, Samyutta Nikaya, II, 3, 8.

Poem XXXII. "Orchid boat" is a metaphor for the female sexual organ.

Poem XXXIII. Echoes Yosano Akiko.

Poem XXXVI. Shoji—sliding doors or windows with "panes" of paper.

Poem XXXVIII. Ono no Komachi (834–880) is certainly Japan's greatest woman poet. Marichiko echoes her most famous poem—"Hito no awan/Tsuki no naki ni wa/Omoiokite/Mune hashibiri ni/Kokoro yakeori."

Poem XL. Echoes the first lines of the Dhammapada, the ancient popular exposition of Theravada Buddhism.

Poem XLI. Echoes an anonymous poem usually attributed to Hitomaro.

Poem XLII. Echoes a Buddhist sutra.

Poem XLIV. There are a great many midaregami, "tangled hair" poems, from an exchange between Mikata and his wife in the *Manyoshu*—eighth century—to the first great book of Yosano Akiko, called *Midaregami*, the early twentieth-century woman poet and still the unequalled poet of modern verse in classical (tanka) form.

Poem XLV. Shizuka Gozen (twelfth century) was a white dress dancer of spectacular beauty who became the lover of Minamoto no Yoshitsune, the tragic hero of the epic of the war between the Taira and Minamoto, which brought to an end the great years of early Japanese civilization. He was the principal general of his brother Yoritomo, and broke the power of the Taira in a series of battles. After Yoritomo outlawed his brother, Shizuka was captured fleeing through the snowbound wilderness on Mt. Yoshino. When Yorimoto and his courtiers were worshipping at the Tsuruga-Oka Shrine at Kamakura, he commanded Shizuka to perform her most famous dance. She refused but was finally forced to dance. Shortly after, she gave birth to Yoshitsune's son, whom Yoritomo murdered. She then became a Buddhist nun and lived to an old age, long after Yoshitsune had been destroyed in his refuge in the far North. She is not a great poet but, with Yoshitsune, one of the tragic figures of Japanese history. Her dance occurs in several Noh plays.

Poem XLVI. Echoes a Buddhist sutra, but also refers to herself as Marichi—Ray of Light—and Dainichi (Vairocana)—The Transcedent Sun.

Poems XLVII–XLVIII. These two poems are factual—D.D.T. exterminated most of the fireflies of Japan, and the Hotaru Matsuri—Firefly Festivals—are no longer held, or even remembered by the younger generation.

Poem LII. Echoes a Buddhist sutra, the poems of Yokobue and her lover in the *Heike Monogatori,* and finally Buddha's Unicorn (often called "Rhinoceros") Sermon.

Poem LIII. Pachinko is a form of vertical pinball—and immense pachinko parlors, crowded with hypnotized players, litter Japan. It is a symbol of total immersion in the world of illusion, ignorance, suffering, and grasping. Wisdom is Prajna— the female consort of a Buddha in esoteric Shingon Buddhism, corresponding to the Shakti, power, the consort of a Hindu god. Note that Prajna is, in a sense, the contradictory of Shakti.

Poem LIV. The first cuckoo in the dawn poem probably dates back before the *Kokinshu,* the second Imperial Anthology. There are many geisha songs that essentially repeat it. But Marichiko says, "was it the moon itself that cried out?" a completely novel last line. The hototogisu does not say "cuckoo," but something like the five syllables of its name, or "horobirete," perishing. It is *Cuculus poliocephalus.*

Poem LV. Echoes a Buddhist sutra.

Poem LVII. The bell cricket is the Tsukutsuku boshi, *Cosmopsal tria colorata.*

As I finish these notes, I realize that, whereas Westerners, alienated from their own culture, embrace Zen Buddhism, most young Japanese consider it reactionary, the religion of the officer caste, the great rich, and foreign hippies. There is however a growing movement of appreciation of Theravada (Hinayana) Buddhism, hitherto hardly known except to scholars in Japan. Marichiko's poems are deeply influenced by Theravada suttas, Tachigawa Shingon, folksongs, Yosano Akiko, and the great women poets of Heian Japan—Ono no Komachi, Murasaki Shikibu, and Izumi Shikibu.

INDEX OF TITLES, FIRST LINES, & AUTHORS TRANSLATED

Poem titles are printed in *italic* type, names of authors translated are in LARGE AND SMALL capital letters.

After Akiko—"Yoru no cho ni," 12
All This to Pass Never to Be Again, 27
An aging pilgrim on a, 35
An hour before sunrise, 19
Asagumori, 8
As I came from the, 65
A single ray in the dawn, 53
As the full moon rises, 4
As the wheel follows the hoof, 72
Autumn covers all the world, 51

Because I can't stop, 72
Because I dream, 58
Bride and groom, 14
Bright in the East, 26

Can I come to you, 10
Chilled through, I wake up, 82
Clustered in the forest around, 40
Come to me, as you come, 56

Did a cuckoo cry?, 79
Did you take me because you loved me?, 78

EKELOF, GUNNAR, 28, 29, 30
Emitting a flood of light, 75
Equation, 30
Every morning, I, 68

Fires, 59
Flowers sleep by the window, 28
Frost covers the reeds of the marsh, 54
FUJIWARA NO TEIKA, 31

Half in a dream, 81
Hototogisu—horobirete, 16
How long, long ago, 76
How many lives ago, 73

I am sad this morning, 69
I cannot escape from you, 9
I cannot forget, 68
If I thought I could get away, 49
I hate this shadow of a ghost, 82
I hold your head tight between, 67
I look around, 31
In the month of great heat, 17
In the park a crow awakes, 77
In your frost white kimono, 12
I pass the day tense, day-, 60
I scream as you bite, 62
I sit at my desk, 49
Is it just the wind, 70
It is the time when, 64
I waited all night, 71
I wish I could be, 62
I wonder if you can know, 32

Just us, 52

Late night, under the, 7
Late Spring, 13
Let us sleep together here tonight, 59
Long past midnight, I walk out, 25
Love me. At this moment we, 66
Lying in the meadow, open to you, 56

Making love with you, 52
MARICHIKO, 47
Midnight, the waning moon, 22

Nerves grind quietly in the
    twilight, 29
New Year, 18
Night shuts down the misty
    mountains, 41
Night without end. Loneliness,
    81
No leaf stirs. I am alone, 38
Nothing in the world is worth,
    66
Now the fireflies of our youth,
    76

Oborozuki, 42
October Mirror, 29
Oh the anguish of these secret
    meetings, 50
Once again I hear, 77
Once I shone afar like a, 78
Only the sea mist, 15
Only truth can explain your
    eyes, 30
On the bridges, 57
On the forest path, 8
On the mountain, 73
Orange and silver, 5

Plovers cry in the, 24

Scorched with love, the cicada,
    58
Seven Seven, 10
Some day in six inches of, 67
Spring is early this year, 65

The cuckoo's call, though, 16
The disorder of my hair, 74
The drowned moon plunges, 23
The full moon of Spring, 61
The full moon rises over, 37
The full moon shines on, 18
The new moon has reached, 11
The night is too long to the
    sleepless, 80
The uguisu sleeps in the bamboo
    grove, 69
This flesh you have loved, 80
This Spring, Mercury, 61
This world of ours, before we,
    39
Tsukutsukuboshi, 17
Twilit snow, 3
Two flowers in a letter, 74

Uguisu sing in the blossoming
    trees, 55
Under the half moon, 6

Void Only, 9

We feed the blue jays, 27
When in the Noh theater, 75
Who is there? Me, 60
Who was this princess under,
    36
Without me you can only, 79

YOSANO AKIKO, 32
You ask me what I thought
    about, 51
Your tongue thrums and
    moves, 63
You wake me, 54